BIG BOLD BEAUTIFUL ME

BY JANE YOLEN AND
MADDISON STEMPLE-PIATT

ILLUSTRATED BY
CHLOE BURGETT

Magination Press · Washington, DC
American Psychological Association

To my co-author MJSP, first grandchild who taught me everything about being a good Nana, in a bigly way—**JY**

To Violet, Luke, and Landyn Calderone, may you never stop growing Big and Bold—**MSP**

To my boulder-moving husband, my perfect, steady hug—**CB**

Text copyright © 2022 by Jane Yolen and Maddison Stemple-Piatt. Illustrations copyright © 2022 by Chloe Burgett. Published in 2022 by Magination Press, an imprint of the American Psychological Association.

Magination Press is a registered trademark of the American Psychological Association. Order books at maginationpress.org, or call 1-800-374-2721.

Book design by Rachel Ross
Printed by Phoenix Color, Hagerstown, MD

Library of Congress Cataloging-in-Publication Data
Names: Yolen, Jane, author. | Stemple-Piatt, Maddison, author. | Burgett, Chloe, illustrator.
Title: Big bold beautiful me/by Jane Yolen and Maddison Stemple-Piatt; illustrated by Chloe Burgett.
Description: Washington, DC: Magination Press, [2022] | "American Psychological Association." | Summary: This empowering story gets kids cheering for their own wonderful selves and soon realizing that every body is beautiful!
Identifiers: LCCN 2021060572 (print) | LCCN 2021060573 (ebook) | ISBN 9781433838644 (hardback) | ISBN 9781433838651 (ebook)
Subjects: CYAC: Stories in rhyme. | Self-acceptance—Fiction. | Self-confidence—Fiction. | LCGFT: Stories in rhyme. | Picture books.
Classification: LCC PZ8.3.S82285 Bi 2022 (print) | LCC PZ8.3.S82285 (ebook) | DDC [E]—dc23
LC record available at https://lccn.loc.gov/2021060572
LC ebook record available at https://lccn.loc.gov/2021060573

Manufactured in the United States of America
10 9 8 7 6 5 4 3 2 1

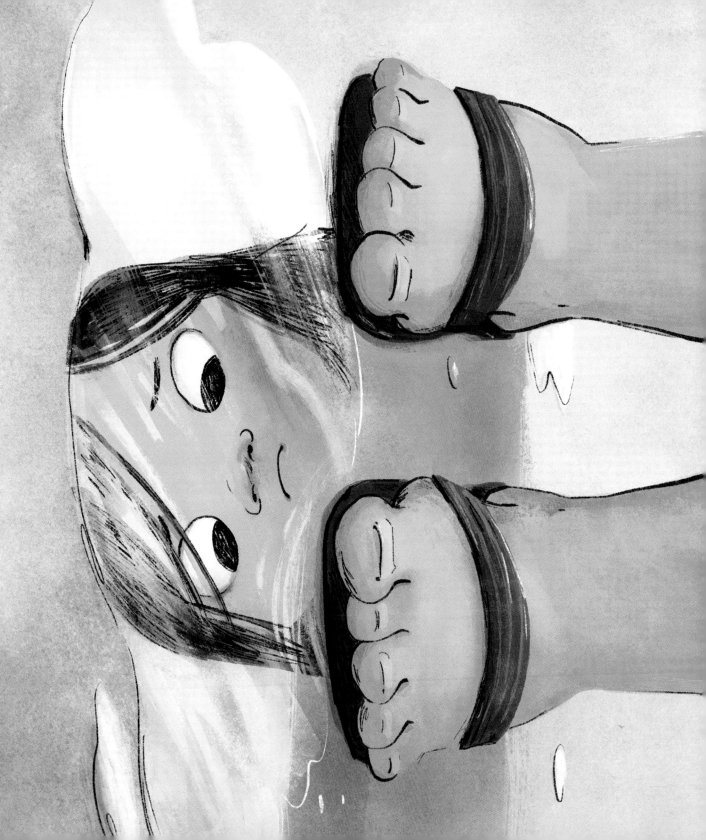

Some folks say I've got peanut butter feet.
And they spread—when I walk—all over the street.

But really they help me
stand steady like Dad,
and upright, too, so
that's not so bad!

I look in the mirror and what do I see?

Some kids gawk at my legs and my thighs.

'cause they're thick like columns that reach to the skies.

But they help me jump,

even higher than my sister.

And walk for causes like a grown-up resister.

When I look in the mirror,
what do I see?

Some friends mention my very broad shoulders.

Say I'd make small work of mighty big boulders.

But I pull my shoulders back, and I walk with pride.

Hiking with my Nana,
going stride for stride.

Then I look in the mirror—
and what do I see?

BIG and BOLD and BEAUTIFUL ME

Some kids at school point out my long arms,

cartwheeling about like windmills on farms.

But Mama's are long, and her hugs are, too.

Anyone who knows her, they know that's true.

Then I look in the mirror—and what do I see?

BIG and BOLD and BEAUTiFUL ME.

I've got untamed curls, boundless and free—

a little like Einstein, or Madame Curie.

I'm curious and daring, with a hair tie in my hand.

There's no problem that I tackle

that I cannot understand.

So, when I look in the mirror—what do I see?

Authors

JANE YOLEN is the author of over 400 books for children and adults. Her books, stories, and poems have won many awards, including the Caldecott Medal, two Nebula Awards, two Christopher Medals, three Golden Kite Awards, and the Jewish Book Award. She lives in Hatfield, MA. Visit janeyolen.com, @Jane.Yolen on Facebook, @JaneYolen on Twitter, and @JYolen on Instagram.

MADDISON STEMPLE-PIATT is Jane's first grandchild. She earned her bachelor's in psychology and was also a Seward Fellow in the Scholars program, for which she created and completed an interdepartmental minor to study body image. She taught group fitness classes for eight years, where she had the opportunity to motivate people to work towards body-positive goals. She has her master's in criminology and criminal justice, and is currently a Juris Doctor candidate. She lives in St. Petersburg, FL.

Illustrator

CHLOE BURGETT is a big, bold children's book illustrator and arts mentor living in Nebraska. See more of her art and say hello to her cat, Pencil, at chloebartistry.com and @chloeb. artistry on Instagram.

u Look Beautiful